Around the Globe Goes Soccer Ball

Michele Jeanmarie

Illustrated by Sara Sampa

Archway Publishing books may be ordered through booksellers or by contacting:

Archway Publishing
1663 Liberty Drive
Bloomington, IN 47403
www.archwaypublishing.com
844-669-3957

ISBN: 978-1-6657-4771-4 (sc)
ISBN: 978-1-6657-4772-1 (e)

Library of Congress Control Number: 2023914407

Print information available on the last page.

Archway Publishing rev. date: 08/02/2023

Around the Globe Goes Soccer Ball

Dedication

To Mother Earth

Soccer ball, soccer ball, what do you see?

I see with my little eyes...

Javier kicking soccer ball.
Palm trees swaying.
Birds a-flapping.

That's what I see.
Good old fun!

Soccer ball, soccer ball, what do you see?

I see with my little eyes...

Gleeful soccer ball.
Fields of flowers.
Insects a-buzzing.

That's what I see.
Grand old fun!

Soccer ball, soccer ball, what do you see?
I see with my little eyes...

Cheerful soccer ball.
Beautiful green grass.
Birds a-flying.

That's what I see.
Peaceful fun!

soccer ball, soccer ball,
what do you see?

I see with my little eyes...

Tearful soccer ball.
Hunters shooting.
Animals dying.

That's what I see.
Poaching!

5

Soccer ball, soccer ball, what do you see?

I see with my little eyes...

Trapped soccer ball.
Fish, fish, and more fish.
Ships and fish galore.

That's what I see.
Overfishing!

Soccer ball, soccer ball, what do you see?

I see with my little eyes...

Petrified soccer ball.
Trees falling down.
Timber trucked away.

That's what I see.
Deforestation!

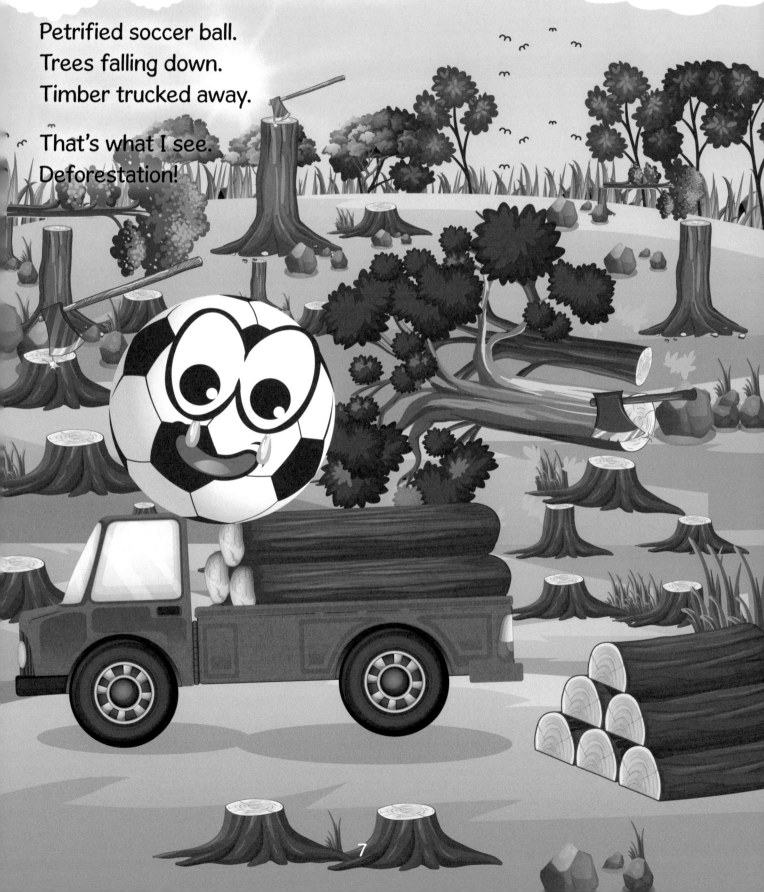

Soccer ball, soccer ball, what do you see?

I see with my little eyes...

Burning soccer ball.
Bushes on fire.
Trees burning.
Water bombing 'copters.

That's what I see.
Wildfires!

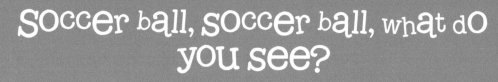

SOCCER ball, SOCCER ball, what do you see?

I see with my little eyes...

Soccer ball straying.
Boats a-drifting.
Bikes a-floating.

That's what I see.
Hurricanes!

9

Soccer ball, soccer ball, what do you see?

I see with my little eyes...

Thirsty soccer ball.
Very parched land.
And dried-up trees.

That's what I see.
Heatwaves!

Soccer ball, soccer ball, what do you see?

I see with my little eyes...

Frowning soccer ball.
Glaciers on the move.
Ice melting.

That's what I see.
Melting ice caps!

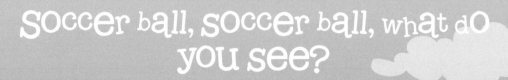

Soccer ball, soccer ball, what do you see?
I see with my little eyes...

Coughing soccer ball.
Fossil burning.
Cars emissions.

That's what I see.
Green house effect!

12

Soccer ball, soccer ball, what do you see?
I see with my little eyes...

Twirling soccer ball.
Eye of the storm.
Chela running.

That's what I see.
Tornadoes!

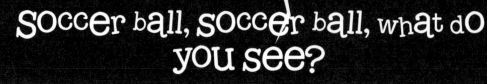

Soccer ball, soccer ball, what do you see?

I see with my little eyes...

Things a-falling.
Buildings collapsing.
Cracks in the ground.

That's what I see.
Earthquakes!

TO scaffOld:

Language and Speaking
Emergent readers:
list what you see on the page

Science
Elementary school children
Explain how each atmospheric change occurred; choose a page and use the five-step scientific method (materials, hypothesis, procedure, theory, {diagram}, conclusion) to demonstrate how each occurred.
Earthquakes are not created by man. Why do think it is here?

Social Studies
Choose a page to...
Describe the interaction between people in your area and how they caused this climate change.
Describe the interaction between people in your area and how they fell victim.

Geography
Describe how your geographical location contributed to or fell victim to one of these climate changes.

Art
The illustrator provided a scenic and happy cover. How was this different to the content? What was her message?

Theology/ Civic
Define stewardship. How can you become a steward of the environment.

Printed in the United States
by Baker & Taylor Publisher Services